This Is the Plate

By Alan Trussell-Cullen
Illustrated by Ruby Barnes

GoodYearBooks

This is the plate.

This is the bread.

This is the jelly.
Spread, spread, spread!

4

Fold it over.

Squeeze it tight.

This is the mouth.

Now, take a bite!

8